FROGGY GETS DRESSED

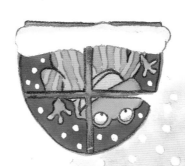

FROGGY GETS DRESSED

by JONATHAN LONDON
illustrated by FRANK REMKIEWICZ

PUFFIN BOOKS

For Sean & Aaron
who love the snow
   —J.L.

For Madeleine
   —F.R.

PUFFIN BOOKS
Published by the Penguin Group
Penguin Putnam Books for Young Readers, 345 Hudson Street, New York, New York 10014, U.S.A.
Penguin Books Ltd, 27 Wrights Lane, London W8 5TZ, England
Penguin Books Australia Ltd, Ringwood, Victoria, Australia
Penguin Books Canada Ltd, 10 Alcorn Avenue, Toronto, Ontario, Canada M4V 3B2
Penguin Books (N.Z.) Ltd, 182-190 Wairau Road, Auckland 10, New Zealand

Penguin Books Ltd, Registered Offices: Harmondsworth, Middlesex, England

First published in the United States of America by Viking Penguin,
a division of Penguin Books USA Inc., 1992
Published in Puffin Books, 1994

40 39 38 37 36 35 34

Text copyright © Jonathan London, 1992
Illustrations copyright © Frank Remkiewicz, 1992
All rights reserved

THE LIBRARY OF CONGRESS HAS CATALOGED THE VIKING PENGUIN EDITION AS FOLLOWS:
London, Jonathan
Froggy gets dressed / by Jonathan London; illustrated by Frank Remkiewicz.
  p. cm.
Summary: Rambunctious Froggy hops out into the snow for a winter frolic
but is called back by his mother to put on some necessary articles of clothing.
ISBN 0-670-84249-4
[1. Frogs—Fiction. 2. Clothing and dress—Fiction. 3. Snow—Fiction.]
I. Remkiewicz, Frank, ill. II. Title.
PZ7.L8432Fr 1992 [E]—dc20 91-45805 CIP AC

Puffin ISBN 0-14-054457-7

Manufactured in China
Set in Kabel

It was cold.
Froggy woke up
and looked out the window.
"Snow! Snow!" he sang.
"I want to play in the snow!"

"Go back to sleep, Froggy,"
said his mother.
"Don't you know?
Frogs are supposed to sleep
all winter. Wake up
when the snow melts."

"No! No!" cried Froggy.
"I'm awake! Awake!
I want to go out and play
in the snow."

So Froggy put on his socks—*zoop!*

Pulled on his boots—*zup!*

Put on his hat—*zat!*

Tied on his scarf—*zwit!*

Tugged on his mittens—*zum!*

And flopped outside

into the snow—*flop flop flop*.

FRRROOOGGYY!

called his mother.
"Wha-a-a-a-t?"
yelled Froggy.
"Did you forget
to put something on?"

Froggy looked down.
"Oops!" cried Froggy. "I forgot
to put on my pants!"

He flopped back inside—*flop flop flop.*

Tugged off his mittens.

Untied his scarf.

Took off his hat.

Pulled off his boots

(he left his socks on)

and slipped his pants on—*zip!*

Then he pulled on his boots—*zup!*

Put on his hat—*zat!*

Tied on his scarf—*zwit!*

Tugged on his mittens—*zum!*

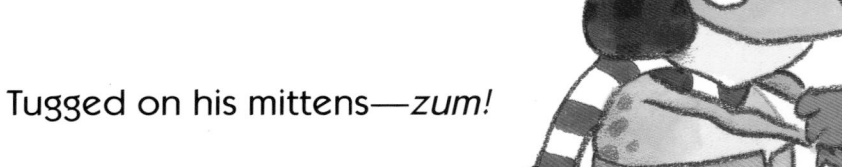

And flopped back outside
into the snow—*flop flop flop.*

FRROOGGYY!

called his mother.

"Wha-a-a-a-t?"
yelled Froggy.
"Did you forget
to put something on?"

Froggy looked down.
"Oops!" he cried. "I forgot
to put on my shirt!"
"*And your coat!*" added his mother.

He flopped back inside—*flop flop flop.*

Tugged off his mittens.

Untied his scarf.

Took off his hat

(he left his pants,

boots, and socks on)

and buttoned up

his shirt—*zut! zut! zut!*

Then he snapped

on his coat—*znap!*

Put on his hat—*zat!*

Tied on his scarf—*zwit!*

Tugged on his mittens—*zum!*

And flopped back outside

into the snow—*flop flop flop.*

FRRROOGGYY!

called his mother.
"Wha-a-a-a-t?"
yelled Froggy.
"Did you forget to
put something on?"

Froggy looked down.

He had on his mittens.

He had on his scarf.

He had on his coat.

He had on his shirt.

He had on his pants.

He had on his boots.

He had on his socks.

He reached up—

Yep! He had on his hat.

What could be missing?

YOUR UNDERWEAR!

His mother laughed.

"Oops!" cried Froggy,
looking more red in the face
than green.

He flopped back inside—*flop flop flop.*

Tugged off his mittens.

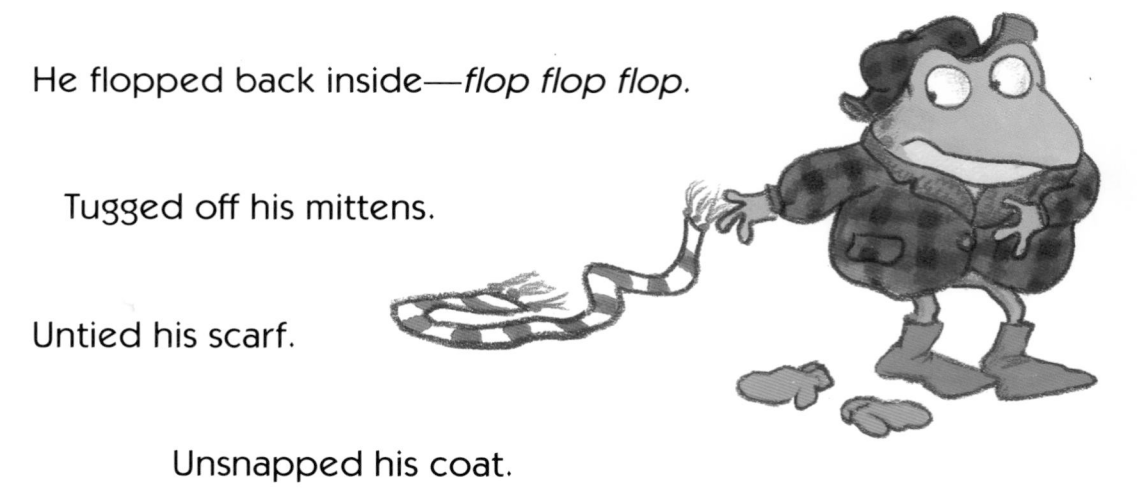

Untied his scarf.

Unsnapped his coat.

Unbuttoned his shirt.

Unzipped his pants.

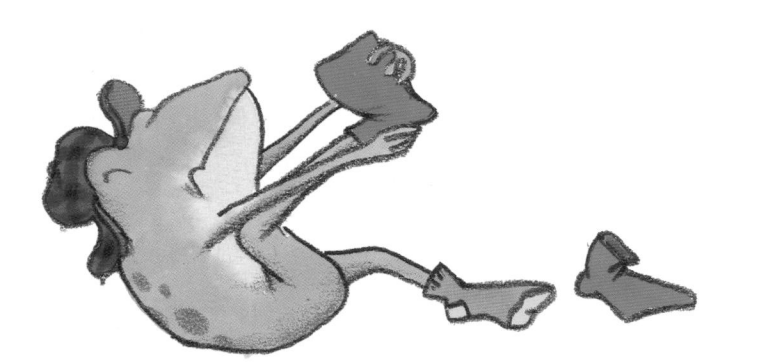

Pulled off his boots.

Took off his socks

(he left his hat on)

and slipped his long johns on—

with a *zap!* of elastic.

Then he put on one sock—*zoop!*

Pulled on one boot—*zup!*

Tugged on one mitten—*zum!*

Started to tug on the other…

...and let it drop.

And said, "I'm too tired."

And went back to sleep.

GOOD NIGHT FROGGY

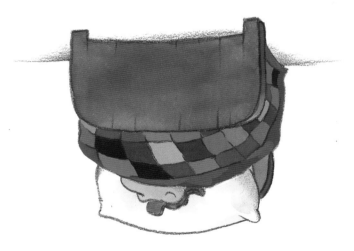

ZZZZZZZZZ